D1528285

Plot Summaries of Shakespeare's Plays: 35 Plays Summarized

CHARLES DUDLEY WARNER

Published by A. J. Cornell Publications

ISBN-10: 149926478X
ISBN-13: 978-1499264784

CONTENTS

5 All's Well That Ends Well

7 Antony and Cleopatra

9 As You Like It

12 The Comedy of Errors

14 Coriolanus

16 Cymbeline

18 Hamlet

20 Henry IV, Part I

22 Henry IV, Part II

24 Henry V

26 Henry VI (Parts I, II, III)

28 Henry VIII

31 Julius Caesar

34 King John

36 King Lear

38 Love's Labour's Lost

41 Macbeth

43 Measure for Measure

45 The Merchant of Venice

47 Merry Wives of Windsor

49 A Midsummer Night's Dream

51 Much Ado about Nothing

53 Othello

56 Pericles

58 Richard II

60 Richard III

62 Romeo and Juliet

64 The Taming of the Shrew

67 The Tempest

69 Timon of Athens

71 Titus Andronicus

72 Troilus and Cressida

74 Twelfth Night; or, What You Will

77 Two Gentlemen of Verona

79 A Winter's Tale

ALL'S WELL THAT ENDS WELL

All's Well That Ends Well is a play, the story of which came to the poet from Boccaccio, through Paynter's *Palace of Pleasure*, although he introduces variations. It tells how Helen de Narbon, a physician's daughter, and orphaned, forced her love on a handsome and birth-proud young French nobleman, Bertram de Rousillon, with whom she had been brought up from childhood. It is a tale of husband-catching by a curious kind of trick. To most *men* the play is repellent. Yet Shakespeare has treated the theme again in *Twelfth Night* (Olivia), and in *Midsummer Night's Dream* (Helena). Many women woo in courtship—by word, glance, or gesture at least; and among the lower orders the courting is quite undisguised. Shakespeare endows Helena with such virtues that we excuse and applaud. All's well that ends well. She heals the king with her father's receipt, asks for and accepts Bertram as her reward, and is married. But the proud boy flies to the Florentine wars on his wedding-day, leaving his marriage unconsummated. Helen returns sorrowfully to Rousillon;

and finds there a letter from her husband, to the effect that when she gets his ring upon her finger and shows him a child begotten of his body, then he will acknowledge her as his wife. She undertakes to outwit him and reclaim him. Leaving Rousillon on pretense of a pilgrimage to the shrine of Saint Jacques le Grand, she presently contrives to have it thought she is dead. In reality she goes to Italy, and becomes Bertram's wife in fact and not mere name, by the secret substitution of herself for the pretty Diana, with whom he has an assignation arranged. There is an entanglement of petty accidents and incidents connected with an exchange of rings, etc. But, finally, Helen makes good before the King her claim of having fulfilled Bertram's conditions; and she having vowed obedience, he takes her to his heart, and we may suppose they live happily together "till there comes to them the destroyer of delights and the sunderer of societies." One's heart warms to the noble old Countess of Rousillon, who loves Helen as her own daughter. She is wise and ware in worldly matters, and yet full of sympathy, remembering her own youth. Parolles is a cross between Thersites and Pistol—a volte-faced scoundrel who has to pull the devil by the tail for a living. His pretense of fetching off his drum, and his trial blindfolded before the soldiers, raises a laugh; but the humor is much inferior to that of *Henry IV*.

ANTONY AND CLEOPATRA

Antony and Cleopatra, written about 1607, is the second of
Shakespeare's Roman plays, *Julius Caesar* being the first.
For breadth of treatment and richness of canvas it excels
the latter. There is a splendid audacity and self-conscious
strength, almost diablerie, in it all. In Cleopatra, the gipsy
sorceress queen, the gorgeous Oriental voluptuousness is
embodied; in the strong-thewed Antony, the stern soldier-
power of Rome weakened by indulgence in lust. There is
no more affecting scene in Shakespeare than the death,
from remorse, of Enobarbus. In the whole play the poet
follows North's *Plutarch* for his facts. The three rulers of
the Roman world are Mark Antony, Octavius Caesar, and
their weak tool, Lepidus. While Antony is idling away the
days in Alexandria with Cleopatra, and giving audience to
Eastern kings, in Italy things are all askew. His wife Fulvia
has died. Pompey is in revolt with a strong force on the
high seas. At last Antony is shamed home to Rome.
Lepidus and other friends patch up a truce between him
and Caesar, and it is cemented by Antony marrying

Caesar's sister Octavia, to the boundless vexation of Cleopatra. What a contrast between the imperial Circe, self-willed, wanton, spell-weaving, and the sweet, gentle Octavia, wifely and loyal! From the time when Antony first met his "serpent of old Nile," in that rich Venetian barge of beaten gold, wafted by purple sails along the banks of the Cydnus, up to the fatal day of Actium, when in her great trireme she fled from Caesar's ships, and he shamefully fled after her, he was infatuated over her, and she led him to his death. After the great defeat at Actium, Enobarbus and other intimate followers deserted the waning fortunes of Antony. Yet once more he tried the fortune of battle, and on the first day was victorious, but on the second was defeated by sea and land. Being falsely told that Cleopatra is dead, Antony falls on his sword. Cleopatra has taken refuge in her monument, and she and her women draw up the dying lover to its top. But the monument is forced by Caesar's men, and the queen put under a guard. She has poisonous asps smuggled in a basket of figs, and applies one to her breast and another to her arm, and so dies, looking in death "like sleep," and "As she would catch another Antony in her strong toil of grace."

AS YOU LIKE IT

In this happiest of his middle-period comedies, Shakespeare is at no pains to avoid a tinge of the fantastical and ideal. Its realism lies in its gay riant feeling, the fresh woodland sentiment, the exhilaration of spirits that attend the escape from the artificialities of urban society. For one reason or another all the characters get exiled, and all meet in the Forest of Arden, where "as you like it" is the order of the day. There is the manly young Orlando, his villainous elder brother Oliver, and their servant Adam. At court is the reigning duke, his daughter Celia, her cousin Rosalind, and Touchstone the clown. In the forest, the banished elder duke (father of Rosalind) and the melancholy Jacques, and other lords who are blowzed with sun and wind a-chasing the dappled deer under the greenwood tree; the pealing bugle, the leaping arrow, the *al fresco* table loaded with the juicy roast of venison, and long idle summer hours of leisurely converse. On the outskirts of the forest are shepherd swains and lasses—old Corin, Silvius (in love with Phebe), and the wench Audrey.

Orlando has had to fly from his murderous brother. Rosalind has been banished from the court by her uncle, and she and Celia disguised as shepherd men have slipped away with Touchstone. Now Rosalind has been deeply smitten with Orlando since she saw him overcome the duke's wrestler, and he is equally in love with her. We may imagine her as "a nut-brown maid, tall, strong, rustically clad in rough forest garments," and possessing a perennial flow of cheerful spirits, a humor of the freshest and kindliest. Touchstone is a fellow of twinkling eye and dry and caustic wit, his face as solemn as a churchyard while his hearers are all agrin. He and Jacques look at life with a cynical squint. Jacques is a blasé libertine, who is pleased when things run counter and athwart with people, but is after all not so bad as he feigns to be. Like a series of dissolving views, scene after scene is glimpsed through the forest glades—here the forester lords singing, and bearing the antlers of the stag: there love-sick Orlando carving verses on the bark of trees, or rescuing his brother from the lion. The youth Ganymede (really Rosalind) pretends she can cure Orlando of his love-sickness by teaching him to woo him as if he were Rosalind, all of which makes a pretty pastoral picture. Anon Touchstone passes by, leading by the hand the captive of his spear, Audrey, who has never heard of poetry; or in another part of the woodland he is busy mystifying and guying the shepherd Corin. Ganymede gets the heartless coquette Phebe to promise that if she ever refuses to wed him (with whom she is smitten) she will wed her scorned and despairing admirer Silvius, and makes her father promise to give Rosalind to Orlando; then retires and comes back in her own garments as Rosalind. The play ends with a fourfold marriage and a dance under the trees.

THE COMEDY OF ERRORS

The Comedy of Errors, by its irresistibly laughable plot (and it is all plot), is perennially popular. It is the shortest of the plays, and one of the very earliest written. The main story is from the *Menaechmi* of Plautus. The Syracusans and the men of Ephesus have mutually decreed death to a citizen of one city caught in the other, unless he can pay a heavy ransom. Aegeon of Syracuse is doomed to death by the Duke of Ephesus. He tells the duke his story—how at Epidamnum many years ago his wife had borne male twins, and at the same hour a meaner woman nearby had also twin boys; how he had bought and brought up the latter; and how he and his wife had become separated by shipwreck, she with one of each pair of twins and he with one of each; and how five years ago his boy and servant had set out in search of their twin brothers, and he himself was now searching them and his wife. Of these twins, one Antipholus and one Dromio live in Ephesus as master and servant respectively, the former being married to Adriana, whose sister Luciana dwells with her. By chance the

12

Syracusan Antipholus and his Dromio are at this time in Ephesus. The mother Aemilia is abbess of a priory in the town. Through a labyrinth of errors they all finally discover each other. Antipholus of Syracuse sends his Dromio to the inn with a bag of gold, and presently meets Dromio of Ephesus, who mistaking him, urges him to come at once to dinner: his wife and sister are waiting. In no mood for joking, he beats his supposed servant. The other Dromio also gets a beating for denying that he had just talked about dinner and wife. In the meantime, Adriana and her sister meet the Syracusans on the street, and amaze them by their reproaches. As in a dream the men follow them home, and Dromio of Syracuse is bid keep the door. Now comes home the rightful owner with guests, and knocks in vain for admittance. So he goes off in a rage to an inn to dine. At his home the coil thickens. There Antipholus of Syracuse makes love to Luciana, and downstairs the amazed Dromio of Syracuse flies from the greasy kitchen wench who claims him as her own. Master and man finally resolve to set sail at once from this place of enchantment. After a great many more laughable puzzles and contretemps, comes Adriana, with a conjurer—Doctor Pinch—and others, who bind her husband and servant as madmen and send them away. Presently enter the bewildered Syracusans with drawn swords, and away flies Adriana, crying, "They are loose again!" The Syracusans take refuge in the abbey. Along comes the duke leading Aegeon to execution. Meantime the real husband and slave have really broken loose, bound Doctor Pinch, singed off his beard, and nicked his hair with scissors. At last both pairs of twins meet face to face, and Aegeon and Aemilia solve all puzzles.

CORIOLANUS

Coriolanus, a powerful drama of Shakespeare's later years (written about 1609), retells from North's *Plutarch*, in terse sinewy English, the fate that overtook the too haughty pride of a Roman patrician—generous, brave, filial, but a mere boy in discretion, his soul a dynamo always overcharged with a voltage current of scorn and rage, and playing out its live lightnings on the least provocation. See his fierce temper reflected in his little boy, grinding his teeth as he tears a butterfly to pieces: "Oh, I warrant how he mammocked it!" Mark his strength: "Death, that dark spirit, in's nervy arm doth lie." "What an arm he has! he turned me about with his finger and thumb as one would set up a top." In battle "he was a thing of blood, whose every motion was timed with dying cries." In the Volscian war, at the gates of Corioli, this Caius Marcius performed such deeds of derring-do that he was nigh worshiped; and there he got his addition of *Coriolanus*. His scorn of the rabble, their cowardice, vacillation, dirty faces, and uncleaned teeth, was boundless. The patricians were with him: if the plebeians rose in riot, accusing the senatorial party of "still cupboarding the viand," but never bearing labor like the rest, Menenius could put them down with the apologue of the belly and the members—the belly, like the Senate, indeed receiving all, but only to distribute it to the rest. Coriolanus goes further, and angers the tribunes by roundly denying the right of the cowardly plebs to a distribution of grain in time of scarcity. The tribunes stir up the people against him; and when he returns from the war, wearing the oaken garland and covered with wounds, and seeks the consulship, they successfully tempt his temper by taunts, accuse him of treason, and get him banished by decree. In a towering rage he cries, "You common cry of curs, I banish you!" and taking an affecting farewell of his wife, and of Volumnia his mother (type of the stern and proud Roman matron), he goes disguised to Antium and offers his services against Rome to his hitherto mortal foe and rival, Tullus Sufidius. The scene with the servants forms the sole piece of humor in the play. But his destiny pursues him still: his worser genius, like the Little Master in *Sintram*, whispers him to his ruin; his old stiff-necked arrogance of manner again appears. The eyes of all the admirant Volscians are on him. Sufidius, now bitterly jealous, regrets his sharing of the command; and when, softened by the entreaties of weeping wife and mother, Coriolanus spares Rome and returns with the Volscians to Antium, his rival and a band of conspirators "stain all their edges" in his blood, and he falls, like the great Julius, the victim of his own willful spirit.

CYMBELINE

Cymbeline was written by Shakespeare late in his life,
probably about 1609. A few facts about Cymbeline and his
sons he took from Holinshed; but the story of Imogen
forms the ninth novel of the second day of Boccaccio's
Decameron. These two stories Shakespeare has interwoven;
and the atmosphere of the two is not dissimilar: there is a
tonic moral quality in Imogen's unassailable virtue like the
bracing mountain air in which the royal youths have been
brought up. The beautiful song "Fear No More the Heat
o' the Sun" was a great favorite with Tennyson. Cymbeline
wanted his daughter Imogen to marry his stepson Cloten, a
boorish lout and cruel villain, but she has secretly married
a brave and loyal private gentleman, Posthumus Leonatus,
and he is banished for it. In Italy one Iachimo wagers him
ten thousand ducats to his diamond ring that he can
seduce the honor of Imogen. He miserably fails, even by
the aid of lies as to the disloyalty of Posthumus, and then
pretends he was but testing her virtue for her husband's
sake. She pardons him, and receives into her chamber, for

safekeeping, a trunk, supposed to contain costly plate and jewels, but which really contains Iachimo himself, who emerges from it in the dead of night; slips the bracelet from her arm; observes the mole, cinque-spotted with crimson, on her breast; and notes down in his book the furniture and ornaments of the room. He returns to Italy. Posthumus despairingly yields himself beaten, and writes to his servant Pisanio to kill Imogen; to facilitate the deed, he sends her word to meet him at Milford Haven. Thither she flies with Pisanio, who discloses all, gets her to disguise herself in men's clothes and seek to enter the service of Lucius, the Roman ambassador. She loses her way, and arrives at the mountain cave in Wales where dwell, unknown to her, her two brothers, Guiderius and Arviragus, stolen in infancy. Imogen is hospitably received by them under the name of Fidele. While they are at the chase she partakes of a box of drugged medicine which the wicked queen had prepared, and sinks into a trance resembling death. Her brothers sing her requiem. In the end Cloten is killed, the paternity of the youths revealed, Iachimo confesses his crime, and Imogen recovers both her husband and her brothers.

HAMLET

Hamlet is Shakespeare's longest and most famous play. It draws when acted as full a house today as it ever did. It is the drama of the intellect, of the soul, of man, of domestic tragedy. Five quarto editions appeared during the poet's life, the first in 1603. The story, Shakespeare got from an old black-letter quarto, *The Historie of Hamblet,* translated from the French of Belleforest, who in turn translated it from the Danish History of Saxo Grammaticus. Some time in winter ("'tis bitter cold"), the scene opens on a terrace in front of the castle of Kronberg in Elsinore, Denmark. The ghost of his father appears to Hamlet—moody and depressed over his mother's marriage with Claudius, her brother-in-law. Hamlet learns from his father the fatal secret of his death at the hands of Claudius. He devises the court-play as a trap in which to catch his uncle's conscience; breaks his engagement with Ophelia; kills the wary old counselor Polonius; and is sent off to England under the escort of the treacherous courtiers Rosencrantz and Guildenstern, to be put to death. On the way he rises in the night, unseals their murderous commission, rewrites it, and seals it with his father's ring, having worded it so that they themselves shall be the victims when they reach England. In a fight with pirates Hamlet boards their ship, and is conveyed by them back to Denmark, where he tells his adventures to his faithful friend Horatio. At Ophelia's grave he encounters Laertes, her brother; and presently, in a fencing bout with him, is killed by Laertes' poisoned sword, but not before he has stabbed his treacherous uncle and forced the fatal cup of poison down his throat. His mother Gertrude has just died from accidentally drinking the same poison, prepared by the King for Hamlet. The old threadbare question, "Was Hamlet insane?" is hardly an open question nowadays. The verdict is that he was not. The strain upon his nerves of discovering his father's murderer, yet in such a manner that he could not prove it (i.e., by the agency of a ghost), was so great that he verges on insanity, and this suggests to him the feigning of it. But if you deprive him wholly of reason, you destroy our interest in the play.

HENRY IV, PART I

Henry IV, Part I stands at the head of all Shakespeare's historical comedies, as Falstaff is by far his best humorous character. The two parts of the drama were first published in 1598 and 1600 respectively, the source-texts for both being Holinshed's *Chronicles* and the old play, *The Famous Victories of Henry the Fifth*. The contrasted portraits of the impetuous Hotspur (Henry Percy) and the chivalric Prince Henry in Part I are masterly done. King Henry, with the crime of Richard II's death on his conscience, was going on a crusade, to divert attention from himself; but Glendower and Hotspur give him his hands full at home. Hotspur has refused to deliver up certain prisoners taken on Holmedon field: "My liege, I did deny no prisoners," he says in the well-known speech painting to the life the perfumed dandy on the field of battle. However, the Percys revolt from the too haughty monarch; and at Shrewsbury the Hotspur faction, greatly outnumbered by the King's glittering host, is defeated, and Percy himself slain by Prince Harry. For the humorous portions we have first the broad talk of the carriers in the inn-yard at Rochester; then the night robbery at Gadshill, where old Jack frets like a gummed varlet, and lards the earth with perspiration as he seeks his horse hidden by Bardolph behind a hedge. Prince Hal and Poins rob the robbers. Falstaff and his men hack their swords, and tickle their noses with grass to make them bleed. Then after supper, at the Boar's Head, in slink the disappointed Falstaffians, and Jack regales the Prince and Poins with his amusing whoppers about the dozen or so of rogues in Kendal green that set upon them at Gadshill. Hal puts him down with a plain tale. Great hilarity all around. Hal and Jack are in the midst of a mutual mock-judicial examination when the sheriff knocks at the door. The fat knight falls asleep behind the arras, and has his pockets picked by the Prince. Next day the latter has the money paid back, and he and Falstaff set off for the seat of war, Jack marching by Coventry with his regiment of tattered prodigals. Attacked by Douglas in the battle, Falstaff falls, feigning death. He sees the Prince kill Hotspur, and afterwards rises, gives the corpse a fresh stab, lugs it off on his back, and swears he and Hotspur fought a good hour by Shrewsbury clock, and that he himself killed him. The prince magnanimously agrees to gild the lie with the happiest terms he has, if it will do his old friend any grace.

HENRY IV, PART II

Henry IV, Part II forms a dramatic whole with the preceding. The serious parts are more of the nature of dramatized chronicle; but the humorous scenes are fully as delightful and varied as in the first part. Hotspur is dead, and King Henry is afflicted with insomnia and nearing his end. "Uneasy lies the head that wears a crown," he says in the fine apostrophe to sleep. At Gaultree Forest his son Prince John tricks his enemies into surrender, and sends the leaders to execution. The deathbed speeches of the King and Prince Henry are deservedly famous. All the low-comedy characters reappear in this sequel. Dame Quickly appears, with officers Snare and Fang, to arrest Falstaff, who has put all her substance into that great belly of his. In Part I we found him already in her debt: for one thing, she had bought him a dozen shirts to his back. Further, sitting in the Dolphin chamber by a sea-coal fire, had he not sworn upon a parcel-gilt goblet to marry her? But the merry old villain deludes her still more, and she now pawns her plate and tapestry for him. Now enter Prince

Hal and Poins from the wars, and ribald and coarse are the scenes unveiled. Dame Quickly has deteriorated: in the last act of this play she is shown being dragged to prison with Doll Tearsheet, to answer the death of a man at her inn. The accounts of the trull Doll, and her billingsgate talk with Pistol, are too unsavory to be entirely pleasant reading; and one gladly turns from the atmosphere of the slums to the fresh country air of Gloucestershire, where, at Justice Shallow's manse, Falstaff is "pricking down" his new recruits—Mouldy, Feeble, Wart, etc. Shallow is like a forked radish with a beard carved on it, or a man made out of a cheese-paring. He is given to telling big stories about what a wild rake he was at Clement's Inn in his youth. Sir John swindles the poor fellow out of a thousand pounds. But listen to Shallow: "Let me see, Davy; let me see, Davy; let me see." "Sow the headland with red wheat, Davy." "Let the smith's note for shoeing and plough-irons be cast and paid." "Nay, Sir John, you shall see my orchard, where, in an arbor, we shall eat a last year's pippin of my own graffing, with a dish of caraways and so forth." Amid right merry chaffing and drinking enters Pistol with news of the crowning of Henry V. "Away, Bardolph! saddle my horse; we'll ride all night; boot, boot, Master Shallow, I know the King is sick for me," shouts old Jack. Alas for his hopes! he and his companions are banished the new King's presence, although provided with the means to live.

HENRY V

Henry V is the last of Shakespeare's ten great war dramas. It was first printed in 1600, the materials being derived from Holinshed and the old play on the same subject. Henry IV is dead, and bluff King Hal is showing himself to be every inch a king. His claim to the crown of France is solemnly sanctioned. The Dauphin has sent him his merry mock of tennis balls, and got his stern answer. The traitors—Cambridge, Scroop, and Grey—have been sent to their death. The choice youth of England (and some riff-raff, too, such as Bardolph, Nym, and Pistol) have embarked at Southampton, and the threaden sails have drawn the huge bottoms through the sea to France. The third act opens in the very heat of an attack upon the walls of the seaport of Harfleur, and King Harry is urging on his men in that impassioned speech—"Once more unto the breach, dear friends"—which thrills the heart like a slogan in battle. We also catch glimpses of the army in Picardy, and finally see it on the eve of Agincourt. The night is rainy and dark; the hostile camps are closely joined. King

Henry, cheerful and strong, goes disguised through his camp, and finds that whatever the issue of the war may be, he is expected to bear all the responsibility. A private soldier—Williams—impeaches the King's good faith, and the disguised Henry accepts his glove as a gauge and challenge for the morrow. Day dawns, the fight is on, the dogged English win the day. Then, as a relief to his nerves, Henry has his bit of fun with Williams, who has sworn to box the ear of the man caught wearing the mate of his glove. The wooing by King Henry of Kate, the French King's daughter, ends the play. But all through the drama runs also a comic vein. The humorous characters are Pistol—now married to Nell Quickly—Bardolph, Nym, and Fluellen. Falstaff, his heart "fracted and corroborate" by the King's casting of him off, and babbling o' green fields, has "gone to Arthur's bosom." His followers are off for the wars. At Harfleur, Bardolph, of the purple and bubukled nose, cries, "On to the breach!" very valorously, but is soon hanged for robbing a church. Le grand Capitaine Pistol so awes a poor Johnny Crapaud of a prisoner that he offers him two hundred crowns in ransom. Pistol fires off some stinging bullets of wit at the Saint Tavy's day leek in the cap of Fluellen, who presently makes him eat a leek, giving him the cudgel over the head for sauce. The blackguard hies him home to London to swear he got his scalp wound in the wars.

HENRY VI (PARTS I, II, III)

Of the eight closely linked Shakespeare historical plays, these three are the last but one. The eight cover nearly all of the fifteenth century in this order: *Richard II; Henry IV, Parts I and II; Henry V; Henry VI (three parts);* and *Richard III*—Henry IV grasped the crown from Richard II, the rightful owner, and became the founder of the house of Lancaster. About 1455 began the Wars of the Roses. (The Lancastrians wore as a badge the white rose, the Yorkists the red; Shakespeare gives the origin of the custom in Henry VI, Part I, Act II, Scene 4, adherents of each party chancing in the Temple Garden, London, to pluck each a rose of this color or that as symbol of his adherency.) In 1485 the Lancastrian Henry VII, the conqueror of Richard III, ended these disastrous wars, and reconciled the rival houses by marriage with Elizabeth of York. The three parts of *Henry VI*, like *Richard II*, present a picture of a king too weak-willed to properly defend the dignity of the throne. They are reeking with blood and echoing with the clash of arms. They are sensationally and bombastically written, and such parts of them as are by Shakespeare are known to be his earliest work. In Part I the scene lies chiefly in France, where the brave Talbot and Exeter and the savage York and Warwick are fighting the French. Joan of Arc is here represented by the poet (who only followed English chronicle and tradition) as a charlatan, a witch, and a strumpet. The picture is an absurd caricature of the truth. In Part II the leading character is Margaret, whom the Duke of Suffolk has brought over from France and married to the weak and nerveless poltroon King Henry VI, but is himself her guilty lover. He and Buckingham and Margaret conspire successfully against the life of the Protector, Duke Humphrey, and Suffolk is killed during the rebellion of Jack Cade—an uprising of the people which the play merely burlesques. Part III is taken up with the horrible murders done by fiendish Gloster (afterward Richard III), the defeat and imprisonment of Henry VI and his assassination in prison by Gloster, and the seating of Gloster's brother Edward (IV) on the throne. The brothers, including Clarence, stab Queen Margaret's son and imprison her. She appears again as a subordinate character in *Richard III*. In 1476 she renounced her claim to the throne and returned to the Continent.

HENRY VIII

Henry VIII, a historical drama by Shakespeare, is based on Edward Hall's *Union of the Families of Lancaster and York,* Holinshed's *Chronicles,* and Fox's *Acts and Monuments of the Church.* The key idea is the mutability of earthly grandeur, and by one or another turn of Fortune's wheel, the overthrow of the mighty—i.e., of the Duke of Buckingham, of Cardinal Wolsey, and of Queen Katharine. The action covers a period of sixteen years, from the Field of the Cloth of Gold, in 1520, described in the opening pages, to the death of Queen Katharine in 1536. It is the trial and divorce of this patient, queenly, and unfortunate woman, that forms the main subject of the drama. She was the daughter of Ferdinand and Isabella of Castile, and born in 1485. She had been married when seventeen to Arthur, eldest son of Henry VII. Arthur lived only five months after his marriage, and when at seventeen years Henry VIII came to the throne (that "most hateful ruffian and tyrant"), he married Katharine, then twenty-four. She bore him children, and he never lost his respect for her and her unblemished life. But twenty years after his marriage he met Anne Bullen at a merry ball at Cardinal Wolsey's palace, and fell in love with her, and immediately conceived conscientious scruples against the legality of his marriage. Queen Katharine is brought to trial before a solemn council of nobles and churchmen. With fine dignity she appeals to the Pope and leaves the council, refusing then and ever after to attend "any of their courts." The speeches are masterpieces of pathetic and noble defense. In all his facts the poet follows history very faithfully. The Pope goes against her, and she is divorced and sequestered at Kimbolton, where presently she dies heartbroken, sending a dying message of love to Henry. Intertwined with the sad fortunes of the queen are the equally crushing calamities that overtake Cardinal Wolsey. His high-blown pride, his oppressive exactions in amassing wealth greater than the king's, his *ego et rex meus*, his double dealing with Henry in securing the Pope's sanction to the divorce—these and other things are the means whereby his many enemies work his ruin. He is stripped of all his dignities and offices, and wanders away, an old man broken with the storms of State, to lay his bones in Leicester Abbey. The episode of the trial of Archbishop Cranmer is so pathetically handled as to excite tears. He is brought to trial for heresy by his enemy Gardiner, bishop of Winchester, but has previously been moved to tears of gratitude by Henry's secretly bidding him be of good cheer, and giving him his signet ring as a talisman to conjure with if too hard pressed by his enemies. Henry is so placed as to oversee (himself unseen) Cranmer's trial and the arrogant persecution of Gardiner. Cranmer produces the ring just as they are commanding him to be led away to the Tower; and Henry steps forth to first rebuke his enemies and then command them to be at peace. He does Cranmer the high honor of asking him to become a godfather to the daughter (Elizabeth) of Anne Bullen; and after Cranmer's eloquent prophecy at the christening, the curtain falls. The setting of this play is full of rich and magnificent scenery and spectacular pomp.

JULIUS CAESAR

The material for this stately drama, the noblest of
Shakespeare's historical plays, was taken from Plutarch.
The action covers nearly two years—44 to 42 B.C. The
dramatic treatment, and all the splendid portraiture and
ornamentation, cluster around two points or nodes—the
passing of Caesar to the Capitol and his assassination
there, and the battle of Philippi. Of the three chief
conspirators—Brutus, Cassius, and Casca—Brutus had the
purest motives: "all the conspirators, save only he, did that
they did in envy of great Caesar"; but Brutus, while loving
him, slew him for his ambition and to serve his country.
His very virtues wrought Brutus's ruin: he was too
generous and unsuspecting. The lean-faced Cassius gave
him good practical advice: first, to take off Antony too;
and second, not to allow him to make an oration over
Caesar's body. Brutus overruled him: he spoke to the fickle
populace first, and told them that Antony spoke only by
permission of the patriots. The eloquent and subtle
Antony seized the advantage of the last word, and swayed

all hearts to his will. There lay the body of the world-conqueror and winner of hearts, now a mere piece of bleeding earth, with none so poor to do him reverence. Antony had but to hold up the toga with its dagger-rents and show the pitiful spectacle of the hacked body, and read the will of Caesar—giving each citizen a neat sum of money, and to all a beautiful park for their recreations—to excite them to a frenzy of rage against the patriots. These fly from Rome, and, drawing their forces to a head at Philippi, are beaten by Octavius Caesar and Antony. Both Brutus and Cassius fall upon their swords. The great "show" passages of the play are the speech of the tribune Marullus ("O you hard hearts, you cruel men of Rome"); the speeches of Antony by Pompey's statue ("O mighty Caesar! dost thou lie so low?"—"Here wast thou bayed, brave hart."—"Over thy wounds now do I prophesy"); and of Brutus and Antony in the rostrum ("Not that I loved Caesar less, but that I loved Rome more"; and "I come to bury Caesar, not to praise him")—these, together with the quarrel and reconciliation of Brutus and Cassius in the tent at Philippi. Certain episodes, too, are deservedly famous: such as the description by blunt-speaking, superstitious Casca of the night-storm of thunder and lightning and rain (the ghosts, the surly-glaring lion, and other portents); the dispute at Brutus's house about the points of the compass ("Yon grey lines that fret the clouds are messengers of day"); the scenes in which that type of loyal wifeliness, Portia, appears (the wound she gave herself to prove her fortitude, and her sad death by swallowing fire); and finally the pretty scene in the last act, of the little page falling asleep over his musical instrument, in the tent in the dead silence of the small hours of morning, when by the waning taper as he read, Brutus saw the ghost of murdered Caesar glide before him, a premonition of his death on the morrow at Philippi.

KING JOHN

King John is a drama, the source of which is an older play
published in 1591. The date of the action is 1200 A.D.
John is on the throne of England, but without right; his
brother, Richard the Lion-Hearted, had made his nephew
Arthur of Bretagne his heir. Arthur is a pure and amiable
lad of fourteen, the pride and hope of his mother
Constance. The maternal affection and the sorrows of this
lady form a central feature of the drama. Arthur's father
Geoffrey has long been dead, but his mother has enlisted
in his behalf the kings of Austria and of France. Their
forces engage King John's army under the walls of
Angiers. While the day is still undecided, peace is made,
and a match formed between Lewis, dauphin of France,
and John's niece Blanche. The young couple are scarcely
married when the pope's legate causes the league to be
broken. The armies again clash in arms, and John is
victorious, and carries off Prince Arthur to England, where
he is confined in a castle and confided to one Hubert. John
secretly gives a written warrant to Hubert to put him to

death. The scene in which the executioners appear with red-hot irons to put out the boy's eyes, and his innocent and affectionate prattle with Hubert, reminding him how he had watched by him when ill, is one of the most famous and pathetic in all the Shakespearian historical dramas. Hubert relents; but the frightened boy disguises himself as a sailor lad, and leaping down from the walls of the castle, is killed. Many of the powerful lords of England are so infuriated by this pitiful event (virtually a murder, and really thought to be such by them), that they join the Dauphin, who has landed to claim England's crown in the name of his wife. King John meets him on the battlefield, but is taken ill, and forced to retire to Swinstead Abbey. He has been poisoned by a monk, and dies in the orchard of the abbey in great agony. His right-hand man in his wars and in counsel has been a bastard son of Richard I, by Lady Faulconbridge. The bastard figures conspicuously in the play as braggart and ranter; yet he is withal brave and patriotic to the last. Lewis, the dauphin, it should be said, makes peace and retires to France.

KING LEAR

Shakespeare's great drama *King Lear* was written between 1603 and 1606. The bare historical outline of the story of the King he got probably from Holinshed or from an old play, the *Chronicle History of Leir;* the sad story of Gloster was found in Sir Philip Sidney's *Arcadia.* The motifs of the drama are the wronging of children by parents and of parents by children. With the fortunes of the King are interwoven those of Gloster. Lear has she-devils for daughters (Goneril and Regan), and one ministering angel, Cordelia; Gloster has a he-devil for son (Edmund), and one faithful son, Edgar. The lustre of goodness in Cordelia, Edgar, Albany, loyal Kent, and the faithful Fool, redeems human nature, redresses the balance. At the time the play opens, Lear is magnanimously dividing his kingdom between his sons-in-law Cornwall and Albany. But he has already a predisposition to madness, shown by his furious wrath over trifles, his childish bids for affection, and his dowering of his favorite daughter Cordelia with poverty and a perpetual curse, simply for a little willful reserve in expressing her really profound love for him. Blind impulse alone sways him; his passions are like inflammable gas; for a mere whim he banishes his best friend, Kent. Coming into the palace of Goneril, after a day's hunt with his retinue of a hundred knights, his daughter (a fortnight after her father's abdication) calls his men riotous and asks him to dismiss half of them. Exasperated to the point of fury, he rushes out tired and supperless into a wild night storm; he is cut to the heart by her ingratitude. And there before the hovel, in the presence of Kent, the disguised Edgar, and the Fool, insanity sets in and never leaves him until he dies at Dover by the dead body of Cordelia. In a hurricane of fearful events the action now rushes on: Gloster's eyes are plucked out, and he wanders away to Dover, where Cordelia, now Queen of France, has landed with an army to restore her father to his rights. Thither, too, the stricken Lear is borne at night. The joint queens, most delicate friends, lust after Edmund. Regan, made a widow by the death of Cornwall, is poisoned by Goneril. Cordelia and Lear are taken prisoner, and Cordelia is hanged by Edmund's order. Edmund is slain in the trial by combat. Lear dies; Gloster and Kent are brokenhearted and dying; Regan has stabbed herself; Edgar and Albany alone survive. The Fool in *Lear* is a man of tender feeling, and clings to his old comrade, the King, as to a brother. His jests are like smiles seen through tears; they relieve the terrible strain on our feelings. Edmund is a shade better than Iago; his bastardy, with its rankling humiliations, is an assignable cause, though hardly a palliation of his guilt.

LOVE'S LABOURS LOST

Love's Labour's Lost is Shakespeare's first dramatic production, written about 1588 or '89, and has all the marks of immature style; yet its repartees and witticisms give it a sprightly cast, and its constant good-humor and good-nature make it readable. The plot, as far as is known, is Shakespeare's own. There is an air of unreality about it, as if all the characters had eaten of the insane root, or were at least light-headed with champagne. Incessant are their quick venues of wit—"snip, snap, quick, and home." In a nutshell, the play is a satire of utopias, of all thwarting of natural instincts. Ferdinand, King of Navarre, and his three associate lords, Biron, Dumain, and Longaville, have taken oath to form themselves into a kind of monastic academy for study. They swear to fast, to eat but one meal a day, and for three years not to look on the face of woman; all of which "is flat treason against the kingly state of youth." But, alas! the King had forgotten that he was about to see the Princess of France and three of her ladies, come on a matter of State business. However, he will not admit them into his palace, but has pavilions pitched in the park. At the first glance all four men fall violently in love, each with one of the ladies—the king with the princess, Biron with Rosaline, etc.: Cupid has thumped them all "with his bird-bolt under the left pap." They write sentimental verses, and while reading them aloud in the park, all find each other out, each assuming a stern severity with the perjured ones until he himself is detected. One of the humorous characters is Don Adriano de Armado, "who draweth out the thread of his verbosity finer than the staple of his argument." In him, and in the preposterous pedant Holofernes, and the curate Sir Nathaniel, the poet satirizes the euphuistic affectations of the time—the taffeta phrases, three-piled hyperboles, and foreign language scraps, ever on the tongues of these fashionable dudes. The "pathetical nit," Moth, is Armado's page, a keen-witted rogueling. Dull is a constable of "twice-sodden simplicity," and Costard the witty clown. Rosaline is the Beatrice of the comedy, brilliant and caustic in her wit. Boyet is an old courtier who serves as a kind of usher or male lady's-maid to the princess and her retinue. The loves of the *noblesse* are parodied in those of Costard and of the country wench Jaquenetta. The gentlemen devise, to entertain the ladies, a Muscovite masque and a play by the clown and pedants. The ladies get wind of the masque, and, being masked themselves, guy the Muscovites who go off "all dry-beaten with pure scoff"; Rosaline suggests that maybe they are seasick with coming from Muscovy. The burlesque play tallies that in *Midsummer Night's Dream,* the great folk making satirical remarks on the clown's performances. Costard is cast for Pompey the Huge, and it transpires that the Don has no shirt on when he challenges

Costard to a duel. While the fun is at its height comes word that sobers all: the princess's father is dead. As a test of their love the princess and Rosaline impose a year's severe penance on their lovers, and if their love proves true, promise to have them; and so do the other ladies promise to their wooers. Thus love's labor is, for the present, lost. The comedy ends with two fine lyrics—the cuckoo song ("Spring"), and the "Tuwhit, tu-whoo" song of the owl ("Winter").

MACBETH

Macbeth, one of Shakespeare's great tragedies of passion, which owes its great power of fascination to the supernatural element, was written about 1605. The prose story used was found in Holinshed's *Chronicles*. The somber passions of the soul are painted with a brush dipped in blood and darkness. In every scene there is the horror and redness of blood. The faces of the murdered King Duncan's guards are smeared with it, it stains the spectral robes of Banquo, flows from the wounds of the pretty children of Macduff, and will not off from the little hand of the sleepwalking Lady Macbeth. Banquo and Macbeth have just returned from a successful campaign in the north. On the road they meet three weird sisters, who predicted for Macbeth kingship, and for Banquo that his issue should be kings. 'Tis very late; the owl has shrieked good-night; only the lord and lady of the castle are awake. He, alone and waiting her signal, sees a vision of a phantasmal dagger in the air before him. He enters the chamber. "Hark! it was but the owl."—"Who's there? what ho!"—"I have done the deed: didst thou not hear a noise?" In the dead silence, as day dawns, comes now a loud knocking at the south entry, and the coarse grumbling of the half-awakened porter brings back the commonplace realities of the day. Macbeth is crowned at Scone. But his fears stick deep in Banquo, and at a state banquet one of his hired murderers whispers him that Banquo lies dead in a ditch outside. As he turns he sees the ghost of that nobleman in his seat. "Prithee, see there! behold! look!"— "Avaunt! and quit my sight! Thy bones are marrowless, thy blood is cold; thou hast no speculation in those eyes which thou dost glare with."—"Gentlemen, rise, his Highness is not well." Macbeth, deep in crime, has no resource but to go deeper yet and becomes a bloody tyrant; but ends his career at Dunsinane Castle, where the slain king's sons, Malcolm and Macduff, and ten thousand stout English soldiers, meet their friends the Scottish patriot forces. The tyrant is fortified in the castle. The witches have told him he shall not perish till Birnam wood shall come to Dunsinane, and that no one of woman born shall have mortal power over him. But the enemy, as they approach, cut branches from Birnam wood "to shadow the number of their host." This strikes terror to Macbeth's heart; but relying on the other assurance of the witches, he rushes forth to battle. He meets the enraged Macduff, learns from him that he (Macduff) was ripped untimely from his mother's womb, and so is not strictly of woman born. With the energy of despair Macbeth attacks him, but is overcome and beheaded.

MEASURE FOR MEASURE

Measure for Measure is one of Shakespeare's later tragi-
comedies, the outline of the plot taken from the Italian
novelist Cinthio and from Whetstone's tragedy of *Promos
and Cassandra*. License has now for a long while in Vienna
run by the hideous law, as mice by lions; and the sagacious
but eccentric duke attempts to enforce it, especially against
sins of lust. The scenes that follow are gloomy and painful,
and search deep into the conscience; yet all ends happily
after all. The motif is mercy; a meting unto others, measure
for measure, as we would wish them to mete unto us. The
duke feigns a desire to travel, and appoints as deputies
Angelo and Escalus. They begin at once to deal with sexual
immorality: Escalus none too severely with a loathsome set
of disreputable folk; but Angelo most mercilessly with
young Claudio, who, in order to secure dower for his
betrothed, had put off legal avowal of their irregular
relation until her condition had brought the truth to light.
Angelo condemns Claudio to death. His sister Isabella,
about to enter a nunnery of the votarists of Saint Clare, is

induced to plead for his life. As pure as snow, yet, as her "cheek-roses" show, not cold-blooded, her beauty ensnares the outward-sainted deputy and "seemer," who proposes the release of her brother to her as the price of her chastity. Isabella has plenty of hot blood and moral indignation. She refuses with noble scorn; and when her brother begs his life at her hands, bids him die rather than see her dishonored. The duke, disguised as a friar, has overheard in the prison her splendid defense of virtue, and proposes a plan for saving her virtue and her brother's life too. It is this: There dwells alone, in a certain moated grange, forgotten and forlorn now these five years, Mariana, legally affianced to Lord Angelo, and who loves him still, although owing to the loss of her dowry he has cast her off. The friar-duke proposes that Isabella shall feign compliance, make an appointment, and then send Mariana in her place. Isabella agrees to risk her reputation, and the dejected grass-widow is easily won over to meet Angelo by night in his brick-walled garden. The base deputy, fearing Claudio's revenge if he frees him, breaks his promise and sends word to have him executed. The duke and the provost of the prison send Angelo the head of a prisoner (much like Claudio) who has died overnight: Isabella supposes her brother to be dead. The duke, entering the city gates in state, *in propria persona*, hears her petition for justice. Angelo confesses; and after (by the duke's order) marrying Mariana, is pardoned. Indeed, there is a general amnesty; and the duke takes to wife Isabella, who thus enters upon a wider sphere of usefulness than that of a cloister.

THE MERCHANT OF VENICE

The Merchant of Venice is a drama of Shakespeare's middle period (1594). The story of the bond and that of the caskets are both found in the old Gesta Romanorum, but the poet used especially Fiorentino's *Il Pecorone* (Milan, 1558). An atmosphere of high breeding and noble manners enwraps this most popular of Shakespeare's plays. The merchant Antonio is the ideal friend, his magnificent generosity a foil against which Shylock's avarice glows with a more baleful luster. Shylock has long hated him, both for personal insults and for lending money gratis. Now, some twenty and odd miles away, at Belmont, lives Portia, with her golden hair and golden ducats; and Bassanio asks his friend Antonio for a loan, that he may go that way a-wooing. Antonio seeks the money of Shylock, who bethinks him now of a possible revenge. He offers three thousand ducats gratis for three months, if Antonio will seal to a merry bond pledging that if he shall fail his day of payment, the Jew may cut from his breast, nearest the heart, a pound of flesh. Antonio expects ships home a month before the day, and signs. While Shylock is feeding at the Christian's expense, Lorenzo runs away with sweet Jessica, his dark-eyed daughter, and sundry bags of ducats and jewels. Bassanio is off to Belmont. Portia is to be won by him who, out of three caskets—of gold, silver, and lead, respectively—shall choose that containing her portrait. Bassanio makes the right choice. But at once comes word that blanches his cheeks: all of Antonio's ships are reported lost at sea; his day of payment has passed, and Shylock clamors for his dreadful forfeit. Bassanio, and his follower Gratiano, only tarry to be married, the one to Portia, and the other to her maid Nerissa; and then, with money furnished by Portia, they speed away toward Venice. Portia follows, disguised as a young doctor-at-law, and Nerissa as her clerk. Arrived in Venice, they are ushered into court, where Shylock, fell as a famished tiger, is snapping out fierce calls for justice and his pound of flesh, Antonio pale and hopeless, and Bassanio in vain offering him thrice the value of his bond. Portia, too, in vain pleads with him for mercy. Well, says Portia, the law must take its course. Then, "A Daniel come to judgment!" cries the Jew; "Come, prepare, prepare." Stop, says the young doctor, your bond gives you flesh, but no blood; if you shed one drop of blood you die, and your lands and goods are confiscate to the State. The Jew cringes, and offers to accept Bassanio's offer of thrice the value of the bond in cash; but learns that for plotting against the life of a citizen of Venice all his property is forfeited, half to Antonio and half to the State. As the play closes, the little band of friends are grouped on Portia's lawn in the moonlight, under the vast blue dome of stars. The poet, however, excites our pity for the baited Jew.

MERRY WIVES OF WINDSOR

Merry Wives of Windsor (printed 1602) is a play written at the request of Queen Elizabeth, who wanted to see Falstaff in love. With its air of village domesticity and out-o'-doorness is united the quintessential spirit of fun and waggery. Its gay humor never fails, and its readers always wish it five times as long as it is. The figures on this rich old tapestry resolve themselves, on inspection, into groups: The jolly ranter and bottle-rinser, mine host of the Garter Inn, with Sir John Falstaff and his men, Bardolph, Nym, and Pistol; the merry wives, Mrs. Ford and Mrs. Page, and their families; then Shallow (the country justice), with his cousin of the "wee little face and little yellow beard" (Slender), and the latter's man Simple; further Dr. Caius, the French physician, who speaks broken English, as does Parson Hugh Evans, the Welshman; lastly Dame Quickly (the doctor's housekeeper), and Master Fenton, in love with sweet Anne Page. Shallow has a grievance against Sir John for killing his deer; and Slender has matter in his head against him, for Sir John broke it. But Falstaff and his men outface the two cheese-parings, and they forget their "pribbles and prabbles" in the parson's scheme of marrying Slender to Anne Page. But the irascible doctor has looked that way too, and sends a "shallenge" to Evans. Mine host fools them both by sending each to a separate place for the duel. They make friends, and avenge themselves on the Boniface by getting his horses run off with. Falstaff sends identically worded love-letters to Mrs. Ford and Mrs. Page, hoping to replenish his purse from their husbands' gold. But Pistol and Nym, in revenge for dismissal, peach to said husbands. The jealous Ford visits Falstaff under the name of Brook, and offers him a bag of gold if he will seduce Mrs. Ford for him. Jack assures him that he has an appointment with her that very day. And so he has. But the two wives punish him badly, and he gets nothing from them but a cast out of a buck-basket into a dirty ditch, and a sound beating from Ford. The midnight scene in Windsor Park, where Falstaff, disguised as Herne the Hunter, with stag-horns on his head, is guyed by the wives and their husbands and pinched and burned by the fairies' tapers, is most amusing. During the fairies' song Fenton steals away Anne Page and marries her. The doctor, by previous arrangement with mother Ford, leads away a fairy in green to a priest, only to discover that he has married a boy. And Slender barely escapes the same fate; for he leads off to Eton Church another "great lubberly boy," dressed in white as agreed with Mr. Page. Anne has given the slip to both father and mother, having promised her father to wear white for Slender and her mother to dress in green for the doctor. But she dressed boy substitutes in white and green, and fooled them all.

A MIDSUMMER NIGHT'S DREAM

A Midsummer Night's Dream was written previous to 1598;
the poet drawing for materials on Plutarch, Ovid, and
Chaucer. The roguish sprite Puck, or Robin Goodfellow, is
a sort of half-brother of Ariel, and obeys Oberon as Ariel
obeys Prospero. The theme of this joyous comedy is love
and marriage. Duke Theseus is about to wed the fair
Hippolyta. Lysander is in love with Hermia, and so is
Demetrius; though in the end, Demetrius by the aid of
Oberon, is led back to his first love Helena. The scene lies
chiefly in the enchanted wood near the duke's palace in
Athens. In this wood Lysander and Hermia, and
Demetrius and Helena, wander all night and meet with
strange adventures at the hands of Puck and the tiny fairies
of Queen Titania's train. Like her namesake in *All's Well*,
Helena is here the wooer: "Apollo flies and Daphne leads
the chase." Oberon pities her, and sprinkling the juice of
the magic flower love-in-idleness in Demetrius's eyes,
restores his love for her; but not before Puck, by a mistake
in anointing the wrong man's eyes, has caused a train of

woes and perplexities to attend the footsteps of the wandering lovers. Puck, for fun, claps an ass's head on to weaver Bottom's shoulders, who thereupon calls for oats and a bottle of hay. By the same flower juice, sprinkled in her eyes, Oberon leads Titania to dote on Bottom, whose hairy head she has garlanded with flowers, and stuck musk roses behind his ears. Everybody seems to dream: Titania, in her bower carpeted with violets and canopied with honeysuckle and sweet-briar, dreamed she was enamored of an ass, and Bottom dared not say aloud what he dreamed he was; while in the fresh morning the lovers felt the fumes of the sleepy enchantment still about them. But we must introduce the immortal players of Pyramus and Thisbe. Bottom is a first cousin of Dogberry, his drollery the richer for being partly self-conscious. With good strings to their beards and new ribbons for their pumps, he and his men meet at the palace, "on the duke's wedding-day at night." Snout presents Wall; in one hand he holds some lime, some plaster and a stone, and with the open fingers of the other makes a cranny through which the lovers whisper. A fellow with lantern and thorn-bush stands for Moon. The actors kindly and in detail explain to the audience what each one personates; and the lion bids them not to be afeard, for he is only Snug the joiner, who roars extempore. The master of the revels laughs at the delicious humor till the tears run down his cheeks (and you don't wonder), and the lords and ladies keep up the fun by a running fire of witticisms when they can keep their faces straight. Theseus is an idealized English gentleman, large-molded, gracious, and wise. His greatness is shown in his genuine kindness to the poor players in their attempt to please him.

MUCH ADO ABOUT NOTHING

Much Ado About Nothing was first published in 1600. The mere skeleton of the serious portions of the drama Shakespeare took from Bandello, through Belleforest's translation; the comic scenes are all his own. In the portrayal of Beatrice, Benedick, and Dogberry, he lavishes all his skill. The constable Dogberry is hit off to the life, with his irresistibly funny malapropisms. He is a lovable old heart-of-gold, who is always taking off his hat to himself and his office, and absurdly pardons every crime except the calling of himself an ass. The scene is laid in Messina. Benedick is just home from the wars. He and Beatrice have had some sparring matches before, and thick and fast now fly the tart and merry witticisms between them—she "the sauciest, most piquant madcap girl that Shakespeare ever drew," yet genuinely sympathetic; he a genial wit who tempts fate by his oaths that he will never marry. From the wars comes too Claudio, brave, but a lightweight fop, selfish, and touchy about his honor. He loves Hero, daughter of Leonato. Beatrice is the latter's niece, and in his house and orchard the action mostly takes place. The gentlemen lay a merry plot to ensnare Beatrice and Benedick. The latter is reading in the orchard, and overhears their talk about the violent love of Beatrice for him, and how (Hero has said) she would rather die than confess it. The bait is eagerly swallowed. Next Beatrice, hearing that Hero and Ursula are talking about her in the garden, runs, stooping like a lapwing, and hides her in the honeysuckle arbor. With a strange fire in her ears she overhears how desperately in love with her is Benedick. The bird is limed; she swears to herself to requite his devotion. Hero's wedding-day is fixed: Claudio is the lucky man. But the villain Don John concocts a plot which has most painful results—for twenty-four hours at least. He takes Claudio and his friend Don Pedro to the orchard, and shows them, as it seemed, Hero bidding John's follower Borachio a thousand good-nights: it is really her maid Margaret in her garments. Claudio in a rage allows her to go to church, but before the altar scornfully rejects her. Her father is in despair, Beatrice nobly indignant and incredulous. Hero swoons, and the officiating friar advises the giving out that she is dead from the shock. Claudio believes it, and hangs verses on her tomb. Meantime Dogberry's famous night-watch have overheard Borachio confess the villainous practice of John and himself. Then Hero's joyful friends plan a little surprise for Claudio. Leonato makes him promise, in reparation, to marry a cousin of Hero's, who turns out to be Hero herself come to life. A double wedding follows, for Benedick willingly suffers himself to be chaffed for eating his words and becoming "the married man." Yet both he and Beatrice vow they take each other only out of pity.

OTHELLO

Othello ranks with *Hamlet, King Lear,* and *Macbeth* as one of Shakespeare's four great masterpieces of tragedy. The bare outline of the story came to him from Cinthio's *Il Moro di Venezia*. It is the story of "one who loved not wisely, but too well; of one not easily jealous, but being wrought, perplexed in the extreme." Othello has a rich exotic nature, a heroic tenderness, quick sense of honor, childlike trust, yet fiercest passion when wronged in his soul. In Iago we have a werewolf s face behind a mask of stoutest honesty; he is one to whom goodness is sheer silliness and cruel craft a fine prudence. Othello, the Moor, has wedded Desdemona, and from Venice sailed to Cyprus, followed by Roderigo, who is in love with her and is a tool of Iago. Iago hates Othello for appointing Cassio his lieutenant, leaving him to be his humble standard-bearer. He also suspects him of having cuckolded him, and for mere suspicion in that kind will diet his revenge by trying to pay him off wife for wife, or failing that, to poison his happiness forever by jealousy. And he wants Cassio's place. He persuades Roderigo that Cassio and Desdemona are in love, and that if he is to prosper, Cassio must be degraded from office or killed. The loyal Cassio has a poor brain for drink, Iago gets him tipsy and involved in a fray, and then has the garrison alarmed by the bell. Othello dismisses Cassio from office. The poor man, smitten with deep shame and despair, is advised by "honest" Iago to seek the mediation of the divine Desdemona, and out of this he will work his ruin; for he craftily instills into the mind of Othello that his wife intercedes for Cassio as for a paramour, and brings him where he sees Cassio making his suit to her, but retiring when he perceives Othello in the distance. "Ha! I like not that," says Iago. And then, forced to disclose his thought, he reminds the Moor that Desdemona deceived her father by her secret marriage, and may deceive him; also tells a diabolically false tale of his sleeping with Cassio, and how he talked in his sleep about his amour with Desdemona. Othello had given his wife a talismanic embroidered handkerchief, sewed by a sibyl in her prophetic fury. Iago had often urged his wife Emilia to steal this "napkin," and when he gets it he drops it in Cassio's chamber. The Moor sees it in his lieutenant's hands, and further sees him laughing and gesturing about Bianca, a common strumpet, and is told by Iago that Desdemona and his adventures with her were Cassio's theme. When, finally, the "honest," "trusty" Iago tells him that Cassio had confessed all to him, the tortured man throws his last doubt to the winds, and resolves on the death of Cassio and Desdemona both. Cassio is only wounded; but the gentle Desdemona, who, all heartbroken and foreboding, has retired, is awaked by Othello's last kisses (for his love is not wholly quenched), and after a terrible talk, is smothered by him where she lies—reviving for a moment, after the entrance of Emilia, to assert that Othello is innocent and that she killed herself. The Moor avows the deed, however, both to Emilia and to two Venetian officials, who have just arrived on State business. In the conversation Iago's villainy comes to light through Emilia's telling the truth about the handkerchief; she is stabbed to death by Iago, while Othello in bitter remorse stabs himself, and as he dies imprints a convulsive kiss on the cold lips of Desdemona. Iago is led away to torture and death.

PERICLES

Pericles is a play written in part by Shakespeare. His part in
it begins with the magnificent storm scene in Act III—
"Thou god of this great vast, rebuke these surges,"—"The
seaman's whistle is as a whisper in the ears of death,
unheard," etc. The play was very popular with the masses
for a hundred years. Indeed the romantic plot is enough to
make it perennially interesting and pathetic; the deepest
springs of emotion and of tears are touched by the scenes
in which Pericles recovers his lost wife and his daughter.
After certain strange adventures Pericles, Prince of Tyre,
arrives with ships loaded with grain at Tarsus, and feeds
the starving subjects of King Cleon and Queen Dionyza.
Afterwards shipwrecked by Pentapolis, he recovers from
the waves his suit of armor, and buying a horse with a
jewel, goes to King Simonides's court and jousts for his
daughter Thaisa's love. He marries her, and in returning to
Tyre his wife gives birth, in the midst of a terrible storm,
to a daughter whom he names Marina. The mother,
supposed dead, is laid by Pericles in a watertight

bitumened chest, with jewels and spices, etc., and is thrown overboard by the sailors, but cast ashore at Ephesus and restored to life by the wise and good physician Cerimon. Pericles lands with his infant daughter at Tarsus, where he leaves her with his old friends Cleon and Dionyza. The pretty Marina grows up, and so excites the hatred of the queen by outshining her own daughter, that she tries to kill her; but the girl is rescued by pirates, who carry her to Mitylene, where she is bought by the owner of a disreputable house, but escapes to take service as a kind of companion in an honest family. The fame of her beauty and accomplishments spreads through the city. One festal day comes Pericles, sad and ill, in his ship to Mitylene, and meeting with Marina, learns from her her story. His joy is so great that he fears death. By Diana's command, revealed to him in a vision, he goes to Ephesus to confess before the people and before her priestess the story of his life. The officiating priestess turns out to be his wife Thaisa, who went from the physician's house to become a ministrant in the temple of the goddess of chastity.

RICHARD II

This drama (based on Holinshed's *Chronicle*) tells the story of the supplanting, on the throne of England, of the handsome and sweet-natured, but weak-willed Richard II, by the politic Bolingbroke (Henry IV). The land is impoverished by Richard's extravangances. He is surrounded by flatterers and boon companions (Bushy, Bagot, and Green), and has lost the good-will of his people. The central idea of *Richard II* is that the kingly office cannot be maintained without strength of brain and hand. Old John of Gaunt (or Ghent) is loyal to Richard; but on his deathbed sermons him severely, and dying, prophesies of England—"this seat of Mars": "This fortress built by Nature for herself/Against infection and the hand of war,/This happy breed of men, this little world." Richard lets him talk; but no sooner is the breath out of his body than he seizes all his movable or personal wealth and that of his banished son Bolingbroke, to get money for his Irish wars. This step costs Richard his throne. While absent in Ireland, Bolingbroke lands with a French force, to regain his property and legal rights as a nobleman and open the purple testament of bleeding war. The country rises to welcome him. Even a force in Wales, tired of waiting for Richard, who was detained by contrary winds, disperses just a day before he landed. Entirely destitute of troops, he humbly submits, and in London a little later gives up his crown to Henry IV. Richard is imprisoned at Pomfret Castle. Here, one day, he is visited by a man who was formerly a poor groom of his stable, and who tells him how it irked him to see his roan Barbary with Bolingbroke on his back on coronation day, stepping along as if proud of his new master. Just then one Exton appears, in obedience to a hint from Henry IV, with men armed to kill. Richard at last (but too late) shows a manly spirit; and snatching a weapon from one of the assassins, kills him and then another, but is at once struck dead by Exton. Henry IV lamented this bloody deed to the day of his death, and it cost him dear in the censures of his people.

RICHARD III

Richard III is the last of a closely linked group of historical
tragedies. As the drama opens, Clarence, the brother of
Richard (or Gloster, as he is called) is being led away to the
Tower, where, through Gloster's intrigues, he is soon
murdered on a royal warrant. The dream of Clarence is a
famous passage—how he thought Richard drowned him at
sea; and in hell the shade of Prince Edward, whom he
himself had helped to assassinate at Tewkesbury, wandered
by, its bright hair dabbled in blood, and crying: "Clarence
is come; false, fleeting, perjured Clarence." Gloster also
imprisons the son of Clarence, and meanly matches
Clarence's daughter. The Prince Edward mentioned was
son of the gentle Henry VI, whom Richard stabbed in the
Tower. This hunchbacked devil next had the effrontery to
woo to wife Anne, widow of the Edward he had slain. She
had not a moment's happiness with him, and deserved
none. He soon killed her, and announced his intention of
seeking the hand of Elizabeth, his niece, after having hired
one Tyrrel to murder her brothers, the tender young

princes, sons of Edward IV, in the Tower. Tyrrel employed two hardened villains to smother these pretty boys; and even the murderers wept as they told how they lay asleep, "girdling one another within their innocent alabaster arms," a prayer-book on their pillow, and their red lips almost touching. The savage boar also stained himself with the blood of Lord Hastings, of the brother and son of Edward IV's widow, and of Buckingham, who, almost as remorseless as himself, had helped him to the crown, but fell from him when he asked him to murder the young princes. At length at Bosworth Field the monster met his match in the person of Richmond, afterward Henry VII. On the night before the battle, the poet represents each leader as visited by dreams—Richmond seeing pass before him the ghosts of all whom Richard has murdered, who encourage him and bid him be conqueror on the morrow; and Richard seeing the same ghosts pass menacingly by him, bidding him despair and promising to sit heavy on his soul on the day of battle. He awakes, cold drops of sweat standing on his brow; the lights burn blue in his tent: "Is there a murderer here? No. Yes, I am: then fly. What, from myself?" Day breaks; the battle is joined; Richard fights with fury, and his horse is killed under him: "A horse! a horse! my kingdom for a horse!" But soon brave Richmond has him down, crying, "The day is ours: the bloody dog is dead." The story of Richard III reads more like that of an Oriental or African despot than that of an English monarch.

ROMEO AND JULIET

Romeo and Juliet was first published in 1597. The plot was taken from a poem by Arthur Brooke, and from the prose story in Paynter's *Palace of Pleasure.* The comical under-plot of the servants of Capulet vs. those of Montague; the fatal duels, the deaths of Mercutio and Tybalt; the ball where Romeo, a Montague, falls in love with Juliet; the impassioned love-scenes in the orchard; the encounter of the Nurse and Peter with the mocking gallants; the meetings at Friar Laurence's cell, and the marriage of Juliet there; Romeo's banishment; the attempt to force Juliet to marry the County Paris; the Friar's device of the sleeping-potion; the night scene at the tomb, Romeo first unwillingly killing Paris and then taking poison; the waking of Juliet, who stabs herself by her husband's body; the reconciliation of the rival families—such are the incidents in this old Italian story, which has touched the hearts of men now for six hundred years. It is the drama of youth, "the first bewildered stammering interview of the heart," with the delicious passion, pure as dew, of first love, but love thwarted by fate and death. Sampson bites his thumb at a Montague; Tybalt and Mercutio fall. Friar John is delayed; Romeo and Juliet die. Such is the irony of destiny. The medieval manners at once fierce and polished—Benvenuto limns them. We are in the warm south: the dense gray dew on leaf and grass at morn, the cicada's song, the nightingale, the half-closed flower-cups, the drifting perfume of the orange blossom, stars burning dilated in the blue vault. Then the deep melancholy of the story. And yet there is a kind of triumph in the death of the lovers: for in four or five days they had lived an eternity; death made them immortal. On fire, both, with impatience, in vain the Friar warns them that violent delights have violent ends. Blinded by love, they only half note the prescience of their own souls. 'Twas written in the stars that Romeo was to be unlucky: at the supper he makes a mortal enemy; his interference in a duel gets Mercutio killed; his over-haste to poison himself leads on to Juliet's death. As for the garrulous old Nurse, foul-mouthed and tantalizing, she is too close to nature not to be a portrait from life; her advice to "marry Paris" reveals the full depth of her banality. Old Capulet is an Italian Squire Western, a chough of lands and houses, who treats this exquisite daughter just as the Squire treats Sophia. Mercutio is everybody's favorite: the gallant loyal gentleman, of infinite teeming fancy, in all his raillery not an unkind word, brave as a lion, tender-hearted as a girl, his quips and sparkles of wit ceasing not even when his eyes are glazing in death.

THE TAMING OF THE SHREW

The Taming of the Shrew, partly by Shakespeare and partly by
an unknown hand, is a witty comedy of intrigue, founded
on an old play about "the taming of the shrew" and on
Ariosto's *I Suppositi;* and is preceded by another briefer bit
of dramatic fun (the "induction") on a different topic—
i.e., how a drunken tinker, picked up on a heath before an
alehouse by a lord and his huntsmen, is carried
unconscious to the castle, and put to bed, and waited on
by obsequious servants, treated to sumptuous fare, and
music, and perfumes, and told that for many years he has
been out of his head, and imagining that he was a poor
tinker. "What! am I not Christopher Sly, old Sly's son of
Burton Heath?... ask Marian Hacket, the fat ale-wife of
Wincot, if she know me not." At length this Sancho Panza,
who still retains his fondness for small ale, sits down to see
the laughter-moving comedy *The Taming of the Shrew,*
enacted for his sole benefit by some strolling players. The
brainless sot found its delicious humor dull; not so the
public. Baptista, a rich old gentleman of Padua, has two

daughters. The fair Katharina has a bit of a devil in her, is cursed with a shrewish temper; but this is partly due to envy of the good fortune of the mincing artificial beauty, Bianca, her sister, whose demure gentle ways make the men mad over her. Yet Kate, when "tamed," proves after all to be the best wife. The other gallants will none of her; but the whimsical Petruchio of Verona has come "to wive it wealthily in Padua," and nothing daunted, woos and wives the young shrew in astonishing fashion. The law of the time made the wife the chattel of her husband, otherwise even Petruchio might have failed. His method was to conquer her will, "to kill her in her own humor." He comes very late to the wedding, clothed like a scarecrow, an old rusty sword by his side, and riding a sunken-backed spavined horse with rotten saddle and bridle. His waggish man Grumio is similarly accoutred. At the altar he gives the priest a terrible box on the ear, refuses to stay to the wedding dinner, and on the way to his country-house acts like a madman. Arrived home, he storms at and beats the servants, allows Kate not a morsel of food for two days, preaches continence to her, throws the pillows around the chamber, and raises Cain a-nights generally so that she can get no sleep, denies her the bonnet and dress the tailor has brought, and so manages things as to seem to do all out of love to her and regard for her health, and without once losing his good-humor. In short he subdues her, breaks her will, and makes his supreme; so that at the end she makes a speech to the other wives about the duty of obedience, that would make the "new woman" of our time smile in scorn. Of Bianca's three suitors the youngest, Lucentio, gets the prize by a series of smart tricks. Disguised as a tutor of languages, he gets her love as they study, while his rivals, "like a gemini of baboons," blow their nails out in the cold and whistle. Lucentio at the very start gets his servant Tranio to personate himself, and an old pedant is hired to stand for his father; and while Baptista, the father of Bianca, is gone to arrange for the dower with this precious pair of humbugs, Lucentio and his sweetheart run off to church and get married. The arrival of the real father of Lucentio makes the plot verily crackle with life and sensation.

THE TEMPEST

The Tempest, one of Shakespeare's very latest plays (1611), written in the mellow maturity of his genius, is probably based on a lost Italian novella or play, though certain incidents are borrowed from three pamphlets on the Bermudas and Virginia and from Florio's Montaigne. The scene is said to be laid in the haunted island of Lampedusa in the Mediterranean. In the opening lines we see a ship laboring in heavy seas near the shore of an island, whose sole inhabitants, besides the spirits of earth and air typified in the dainty yet powerful sprite Ariel, are Prospero and his lovely daughter Miranda, and their slave, the deformed boor Caliban, an aborigine of the island. The grave and good Prospero is a luckier castaway than Robinson Crusoe, in that his old friend Gonzalo put into the boat with him not only his infant daughter, but clothes, and some books of magic, by the aid of which both men and spirits, and the very elements, are subject to the beck of his wand. He was the rightful Duke of Milan, but was supplanted by his brother Antonio, who with his

confederate, the king of Naples, and the latter's son Ferdinand and others, is cast ashore on the island. The shipwreck occurs full in the sight of the weeping Miranda; but all hands are saved, and the ship too. The humorous characters are the butler Stephano, and the court jester Trinculo, both semi-drunk, their speech and songs caught from the sailors, and savoring of salt and tar. Throughout the play the three groups of personages—the royal retinue with the irrepressible and malapropos old Gonzalo, the drunken fellows and Caliban, and Prospero with his daughter and Ferdinand—move leisurely to and fro, the whole action taking up only three hours. The three boors, fuddled with their fine liquor and bearing the bark bottle, rove about the enchanted island, fall into the filthy-mantled pool, and are stoutly pinched by Prospero's goblins for theft. The murderous plot of Antonio and the courtier Sebastian is exposed at the phantom banquet of the harpies. Spellbound in the linden grove, all the guilty parties come forward into a charmed circle and take a lecture from Prospero. General reconciliation. Then finally, Miranda and Ferdinand are discovered playing chess before Prospero's cell, and learn that tomorrow they set sail for Naples to be married.

TIMON OF ATHENS

Timon of Athens is by Shakespeare, either in whole or in part. It is a bitter satire on friendship and society, written in the stern sarcastic vein of Juvenal. The sources of the plot seem to have been Paynter's *Palace of Pleasure*, Plutarch's *Life of Antony*, and Lucian's *Dialogue on Timon*. Shakespeare's *Timon* is unique both in his ostentations and indiscriminate prodigality and in the bitterness of his misanthropy after his wealth was gone. Yet he was of the noblest heart. His sublime faith that his friends were as generous as he, and that they were all brothers, commanding one another's fortunes, was a practical error, that was all. Men were selfish wolves; he thought them angels. His bounty was measureless: if a friend praised a horse 'twas his; if one wanted a little loan of £5,000 or so, 'twas a trifle; he portioned his servants and paid his friends' debts; his vaults wept with drunken spilth of wine, and every room blazed with lights and brayed with minstrelsy; at parting each guest received some jewel as a keepsake. When all was gone, full of cheerful faith he sent out to his friends to borrow, and they all with one accord began to make excuse. Not a penny could he get. Feast won, fast lost. The smiling, smooth, detested parasites left him to his clamorous creditors and to ruin. The crushing blow to his ideals maddened him; his blood turned to gall and vinegar. Yet he determined on one last banquet. The surprised sycophants thought he was on his feet again, and with profuse apologies assembled at his house. The covered dishes are brought in. "Uncover dogs, and lap!" cries the enraged Timon. The dishes are found to be full of warm water, which he throws in their faces, then pelts them with stones and drives them forth with execrations, and rushes away to the woods to henceforth live in a cave and subsist on roots and berries and curse mankind. In digging he finds gold. His old acquaintances visit him in turn—Alcibiades, the cynical dog Apemantus, his faithful steward Flavius, a poet, a painter, senators of Athens. He curses them all, flings gold at them, telling them he gives it that they may use it for the bale of man, pronounces his weeping steward the only honest man in the world, builds "his everlasting mansion on the beached verge of the salt flood," where "vast Neptune may weep for aye on his low grave, on faults forgiven," writes his epitaph, and lies down in the tomb and dies.

TITUS ANDRONICUS

A most repulsive drama of bloodshed and unnatural crimes, *Titus Andronicus* was not written by Shakespeare, but probably touched up for the stage by him when a young man. It is included in the original Folio Edition of 1623. No one who has once supped on its horrors will care to read it again. Here is a specimen of them: Titus Andronicus, a Roman noble, in revenge for the ravishing of his daughter Lavinia and the cutting off of her hands and tongue, cuts the throats of the two ravishers, while his daughter holds between the stumps of her arms a basin to catch the blood. The father then makes a paste of the ground bones and blood of the slain men, and in that paste bakes their two heads, and serving them up at a feast, causes their mother to eat of the dish. Iago seems a gentleman beside the hellish Moor, Aaron, of this blood-soaked tragedy.

TROILUS AND CRESSIDA

Troilus and Cressida is one of the later products of
Shakespeare's pen. Whether he got his facts from Chaucer,
or from medieval tales about Troy, is uncertain. The drama
is his wisest play, and yet the least pleasing as a whole,
owing to the free talk of the detestable Pandarus and the
licentiousness of the false Cressid. Some have thought the
piece to be an ironical and satirical burlesque of Homer.
There is very little plot. The young Trojan, Troilus, in love
with Cressida, is brave as a lion in battle and green as a
goose in knowledge of women. (But "to be wise and love
exceeds man's might.") His amour, furthered by Cressida's
uncle, Pandarus, is scarcely begun when Cressida is
exchanged for a Trojan prisoner and led off by Diomed to
the Greek camp. On arriving, she allows herself to be
kissed by the Greek generals, whom she sees for the first
time; as Ulysses says, "There's language in her eye, her
cheek, her lip." She has just vowed eternal loyalty to
Troilus too. But she is anybody's Cressid; and with anguish
unspeakable, Troilus later overhears her making an

appointment with Diomed, and sees her give him his own remembrance pledge. By gross flattery of the beef-witted Ajax, the wily Greek leaders get him to fight Hector. But Hector and he are related by blood, and after some sparring and hewing they shake hands. Hector is then feasted in the Grecian tents. The big conceited bully Achilles, "having his ear full of his airy fame," has grown "dainty of his worth"; and finding his reputation "shrewdly gored" by his long inactivity, and by the praise Ajax is getting, and especially spurred on by the death of Patroclus, at length comes into the field, but plays the contemptible coward's part by surprising Hector with his armor off and having his Myrmidons butcher him. Thersites is a scurvy, foul-mouthed fellow, who does nothing but rail, exhausting the language of vile epithets, and hitting off very shrewdly the weak points of his betters, who give him frequent fist-beatings for his pains. The great speeches of Ulysses, Agamemnon, and Nestor all breathe the selfsame tone of profound sagacity and insight into human nature. They have the mint-stamp of but one soul, and that Shakespeare's. Homer's sketches of the Greek leaders are the merest Flaxman outlines: but Shakespeare throws the Röntgen rays of his powerful analysis quite through their souls, endowing them with the subtlest thoughts. There are no other scenes in Shakespeare so packed with sound and seasoned wisdom as the third of Act I and the third of Act III in *Troilus and Cressida.*

TWELFTH NIGHT; or, WHAT YOU WILL

Twelfth Night; or, What You Will, is a delightfully humorous comedy. An item in the manuscript diary of John Manningham shows that it was played February 2, 1601, in the fine old hall of the Middle Temple, London—a hall still in existence. The twelfth night after Christmas was anciently given up to sport and games; hence the name. The fresh, gay feeling of a whistling plowboy in June was the mood of the writer of *Twelfth Night.* Tipsy Sir Toby's humor is catching; his brain is like a bottle of champagne; his heels are as light as his head, and one feels he could cut a pigeon-wing with capering Sir Andrew "to make all split," or sing a song "to make the welkin dance." The scene is a seaport city of Illyria, where a sentimental young duke is fallen into a love-melancholy over the pitiless lady Olivia. Now the fair Viola and her brother Sebastian—strikingly alike in feature—unknown to each other reach the same city, Sebastian in company with his friend Captain Antonio. Viola enters the service of the duke as a page, in garments such as her brother wore. With the rich

Olivia dwell her Puritanical steward Malvolio, her kinsman
Sir Toby Belch, and her maid Maria, and other servants.
Olivia has a suitor, and Sir Toby an echo, in the lean-
witted Sir Andrew Aguecheek. Malvolio is unpopular: he
thinks because he is virtuous there shall be no more cakes
and ale; but Maria lays a trap for his vanity, which is
fathoms deep. She drops a mysterious letter in Malvolio's
path, penned in Olivia's hand ("her very C's, her U's, and
her T's"). The letter begins with "M.O.A.I. doth sway my
life," bids him be opposite with a kinsman and surly with
servants, recall who commended his yellow stockings and
wished to see him cross-gartered, and remember that some
have greatness thrust upon them. He swallows the bait,
and makes himself such a ridiculous ass that Olivia thinks
him out of his wits, and Sir Toby has him bound and put
into a dark room. Malvolio has called the clown "a barren
rascal," and this keen-witted lovable fellow now has a
delicious bit of retaliation. Assuming the voice of the
curate Sir Topas, he assures him that until he can hold the
opinion of Pythagoras that the soul of his grandam might
haply inhabit a bird, he shall not advise his release. Then
resuming his own voice he indulges in more excellent
fooling. When last seen Malvolio is free, and bolting out of
the room swears he will be "revenged on the whole pack"
of them. To return: Viola (as "Cesario") becomes the
duke's messenger to woo Olivia by proxy. Olivia falls
desperately in love with the messenger; and when
Aguecheek spies her showing him favors, he is egged on
by roguish Sir Toby to write him a challenge. But Cesario
is afraid of the very sight of naked steel, and Sir Andrew is
an arrant coward. Sir Toby, after frightening each nearly
out of his wits with stories of the other's ferocity, at length

gets them for form's sake to draw their swords; when in comes Captain Antonio, and mistaking Cesario for Sebastian, takes his part. In the meantime, Olivia has married Sebastian by mistake for Cesario, and the two knights both get their heads broken through a similar misunderstanding; for however it may be with Cesario, Sebastian is "a very devil incardinate" with his sword. Presently Sebastian and Cesario meet, and the mystery is solved: Viola avows her sex, and marries the duke, whom she ardently loves.

TWO GENTLEMEN OF VERONA

Two Gentlemen of Verona, one of Shakespeare's earliest and least attractive comedies, for the plot of which he was slightly indebted to Bandello, to Sidney's *Arcadia,* and to Montemayor's *Diana Enamorada.* The scene is laid alternately in Verona and in Milan. The noble Valentine of Verona remarks to his friend Proteus that "home-keeping youths have ever homely wits"; hence he will travel to Milan, with his servant Speed. Proteus, a mean-souled, treacherous, fickle young sprig, is in love with Julia, or thinks he is. His servant's name is Launce, a droll fellow who is as rich in humor as Launcelot Gobbo of the *Merchant of Venice.* Julia is the heroine of the piece; a pretty, faithful girl. Proteus soon posts after Valentine to Milan, and at once forgets Julia and falls "over boots in love" with Silvia. Julia also goes to Milan, disguised as a boy, and takes service with Proteus. The latter treacherously betrayed Valentine's plan of elopement with Silvia to the duke her father, who met Valentine, pulled the rope ladder from under his cloak, and then banished him. As in the play of *As You Like It,* all the parties finally meet in the forest, where Valentine has been chosen leader by a band of respectable outlaws. Julia confesses her identity; Valentine, with a maudlin, milk-sop charity, not only forgives Proteus (whom he has just overheard avowing to Silvia that he will outrage her if he cannot get her love), but, on Proteus repenting, actually offers to give up Silvia to him. But Julia swoons, and Proteus's love for her returns. A double marriage ends this huddled-up finale. Launce affines with Touchstone, Grumio, Autolycus, and the Dromios. He is irresistibly funny in the enumeration of his milkmaid's "points," and in the scenes with his dog Crab. This cruel-hearted cur, when all at home were weeping over Launce's departure, and the very cat was wringing her hands, shed not a tear; and when, in Madam Silvia's dining-room, he stole a chicken-leg from the trencher and misbehaved in an unmentionable manner, Launce manfully took a whipping for him. Nay, he stood on the pillory for geese he had killed, and stood in the stocks for puddings he had stolen. Crab enjoys the honor of being the only dog that sat to Shakespeare for his portrait, although others are mentioned in his works.

A WINTER'S TALE

A Winter's Tale, probably the last dramatic piece from
Shakespeare's pen, has the serene and cheerful wisdom of
Cymbeline and *The Tempest*. It is based on Greene's *Pandosto*
(1588). In this story, as in Shakespeare, Bohemia is made a
maritime country and Delphos an island. The name
Winter's Tale derives partly from the fact that the play
opens in winter, and partly from the resemblance of the
story to a marvelous tale told by a winter's fire. Like
Othello, it depicts the tragic results of jealousy—in this case
long years of suffering for both husband and wife, and the
purification of the soul of the former through remorse,
and his final reconciliation with his wronged queen.
Leontes, king of Sicily, unlike Othello, has a natural bent
toward jealousy; he suspects without good cause, and is
grossly tyrannical in his persecutions of the innocent.
Hermione, in her sweet patience and sorrow, is the most
divinely compassionate matron Shakespeare has
delineated. Polixenes, king of Bohemia, has been nine
months a guest of his boyhood's friend Leontes, and is

warmly urged by both king and queen to stay longer. Hermione's warm hospitality and her lingering hand pressures are construed by the king as proof of criminality: he sees himself laughed at for a cuckold; a deep fire of rage burns in his heart; he wants Camillo to poison Polixenes; but this good man flies with him to Bohemia. Leontes puts his wife in prison, where she is delivered of a daughter. He compels Antigonus to swear to expose it in a desert place, and then proceeds with the formal trial of his wife. His messengers to Delphi report her guiltless. She swoons away, and Paulina gives out that she is dead. But she is secretly conveyed away, after the funeral, and revived. Her little son dies from grief. Sixteen years now elapse, and we are across seas in Bohemia, near the palace of Polixenes, and near where Hermione's infant daughter was exposed, but rescued (with a bundle containing rich bearing cloth, gold, jewels, etc.) by an old shepherd. Antigonus and his ship's crew were all lost, so no trace of the infant could be found. But here she is, the sweetest girl in Bohemia and named Perdita ("the lost one"). A sheep-shearing feast at the old shepherd's cottage is in progress. His son has gone for sugar and spices and rice, and had his pocket picked by that rogue of rogues, that snapper-up of unconsidered trifles, Autolycus. The dainty Perdita moves about under the green trees as the hostess of the occasion, giving to each guest a bunch of sweet flowers and a welcome. Polixenes and Camillo are here in disguise, to look after Polixenes's son Florizel. After dancing, and some songs from peddler Autolycus, Florizel and Perdita are about to be betrothed when Polixenes discovers himself and threatens direst punishment to the rustics. The lovers fly to Sicily, with a feigned story for the ear of Leontes; and the old shepherd and his son get aboard Florizel's ship to show the bundle and "fairy gold" found with Perdita, expecting thus to save their lives by proving that they are not responsible for her doings. Polixenes and Camillo follow the fugitives, and at Leontes's court is great rejoicing at the discovery of the king's daughter; which joy is increased tenfold by Paulina, who restores Hermione to her repentant husband's arms. Her device for gradually and gently possessing him of the idea of Hermione's being alive, is curious and shrewd. She gives out that she has in her gallery a marvelous statue of Hermione by Julio Romano, so recently finished that the red paint on the lips is yet wet. When the curtain is drawn by Paulina, husband and daughter gaze greedily on the statue, and to their amazement it is made to step down from its pedestal and speak. They perceive it to be warm with life, and to be indeed Hermione herself—let us hope, to have less strain on her charity thereafter.

ABOUT THE AUTHOR

Charles Dudley Warner (1829–1900) was an American author, editor, and lecturer. Other works include *The Gilded Age: A Tale of Today* (co-authored with Mark Twain), *My Summer in a Garden*, and *As We Were Saying*.

70094772R00046

Made in the USA
Middletown, DE
25 September 2019